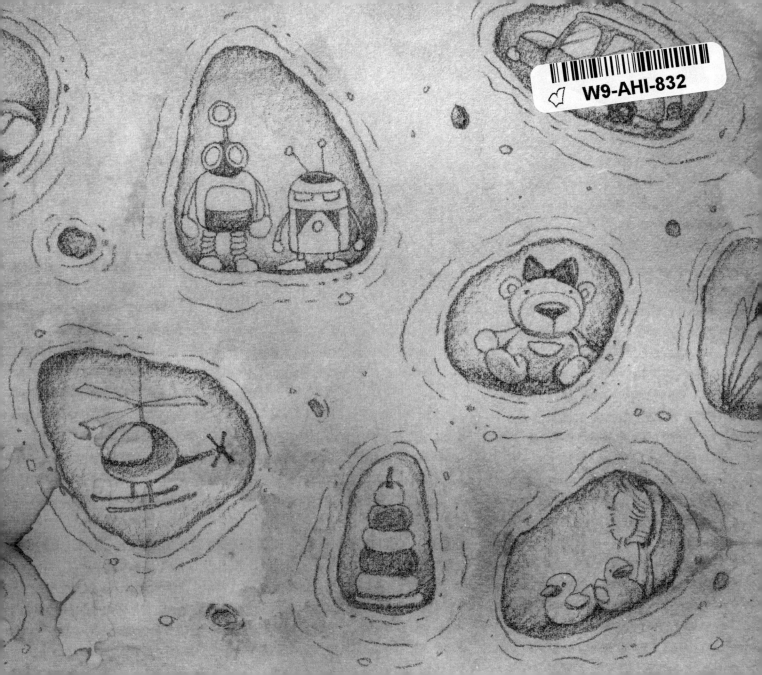

From wonder into wonder existence opens.

Lao Tzu

for Alan McCormick

© 2016 Warren K. Ross, Jr
Wellesley, MA, USA
www.wross.com
w@wross.com

Printed in Shenzhen, China

Publisher's Cataloging-in-Publication Data

Ross, Warren, 1953-
A whole nuther thing / Warren Ross ;
Jade Fang, illustrator.
pages cm
ISBN: 978-0-9903086-1-4 (hardcover)
1. Imagination—Fiction. 2. Persistence—
Fiction. 3. Extraterrestrial beings—Fiction.
4. Picture books for children. I. Fang, Jade,
illustrator. II. Title.
PZ7.1.R67 Wh 2015
[Fic]—dc23

A WHOLE NUTHER THING

by Warren Ross
art by Jade Fang

I crawled in the closet to haul out my truck;
it was gone! In its place was an old hockey puck.
It sure wasn't mine, and it wasn't my mother's;
it wasn't my granny's; it wasn't my brother's.

How did this happen?
We just couldn't say.
But Follansbee came
for a visit next day...

"That's a Hole Nuther thing," he said right away. "I'll tell you the story right now, if I may."

"The Hole Nuther lives in a hole in the ground,
out in the woods near the far side of town.
I've heard people say it's in Dingledong Dell.
But don't bother looking; it's hidden too well.

"Well," I said, "I have
no use for a puck.
How can we get him to
bring back my truck?"

"At night, put out
new things, and
then hit the sack.
He might take a
new thing and put
your truck back."

We put out all kinds of stuff night after night.
I guess for the Nuther, nothing was right.

My cowboy belt buckle, my calaboose latch,
the old watch I found in the blackcurrant patch...

My truck was still missing.
What else could we try?
A cinnamon bun or
a big apple pie?
Inflatable wallaby,
snorkel and flippers?
Supersize Frisbee, my
Squirrel Nut Zippers?

It just wasn't working. I started to mope.
"Don't give up," Follansbee said, "Don't lose hope."
What next? My crayons, my yo-yo, my bike?
Wasn't there SOMETHING the Nuther would like?

Then we tried
something from
Follansbee's mother.
What did she bring us?
She said they were
Druthers.
That night I was tired,
with odd thoughts
in my head.
I fell fast asleep when I
got into bed.

My truck!
It was back!
It looked better than ever...

And that's when I learned to not ever say never.

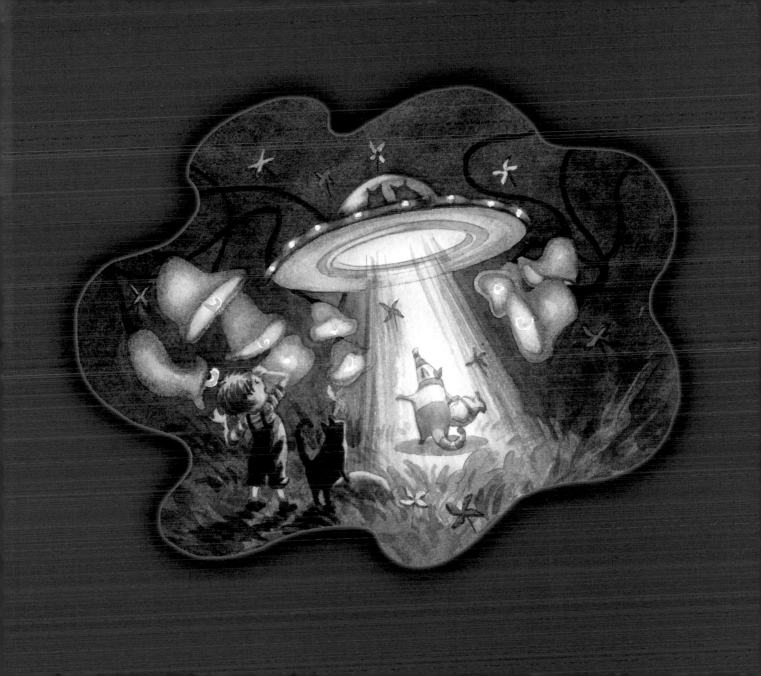

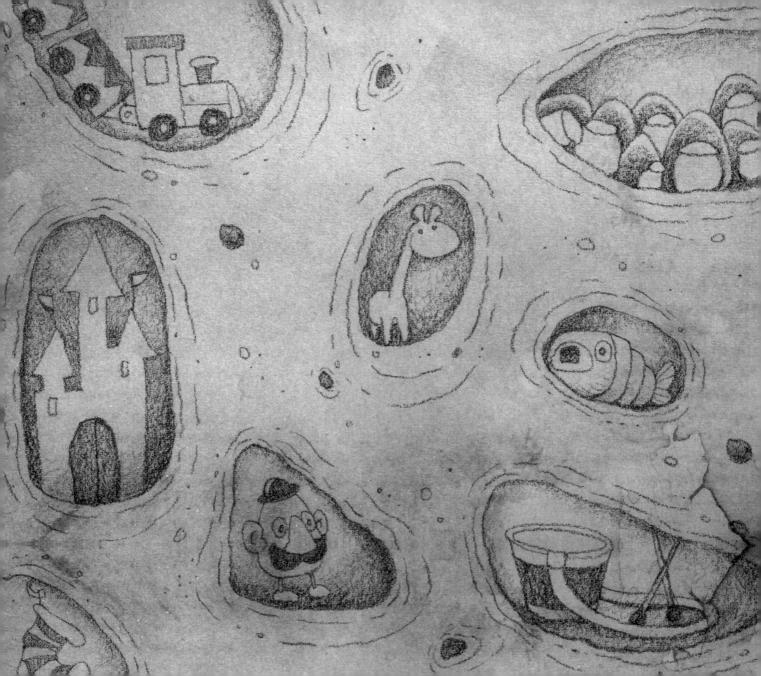